THE DAY IS GONE

This title is number seven in the Frayed Edge Press Street Smart Series

Other titles in the series include:

Full Fare by Jean-Bernard Pouy

Down and Out in Paris, with Cat by R.A. Bolo

The Accidental Anarchist by A.R. Melnik

Stealing MacGuffin by Matthew Kastel

Pele's Domain by Albert Tucher

"Make the Bear Be Nice" by Stephen St. Francis Decky

THE DAY IS GONE

Shelonda Montgomery

Frayed Edge Press
Philadelphia, PA

Copyright 2021

Published by Frayed Edge Press in 2021

https://www.frayededgepress.com/

This book is printed on acid-free paper

Illustrations by graphica013

Publisher's Cataloging-in-Publication Data
Names: Montgomery, Shelonda.
Title: The day is gone / Shelonda Montgomery.
Description: Philadelphia, PA : Frayed Edge Press, 2021. | Series: Street smart
    series ; 7 | Summary: A Chicago family's lives are disrupted when two young
    brothers and their friend discover the body of a local store owner in a ditch,
    setting in motion their mother's plan to move the family to a safer neighborhood.
Identifiers: LCCN 2021944753 | ISBN 9781642510393 (pbk.) | ISBN
    781642510409 (ebook)
Subjects: LCSH: African American families – Illinois – Chicago – Fiction. |
    Family relationships -- Fiction. | Runaway husbands -- Fiction. | Single mothers
    -- Fiction. | Chicago (Ill.) -- Fiction. | BISAC: FICTION / African American
    & Black / General. | FICTION / Family Life / Siblings. | FICTION / Urban
    & Street Lit.
Classification: LCC PS3613 O58 D39 2021 | DDC 813 M66--dc23
LC record available at https://lccn.loc.gov/2021944753

The Ditch

"He dead?"

"Don't know."

"Looks dead to me."

"Lips all purple like he dead. Eyes open," Walter says, eating a red freeze-pop which is now just juice.

He and Earl look at Charlie Jackson, a man from their neighborhood. Walter's little brother Lawrence sits on the gate and tries to stretch his neck so he can see. Walter lets the freeze-pop go. It hangs from his lips. Charlie's body lies in the ditch, his mouth and eyes open. A bloody sheet covers half of his naked body. His chest and head are out and flies swarm around his open eyes and mouth, buzzing loud.

Charlie owned a grocery store that sells a bunch of the usual things: bread, butter, cold cuts, hog head cheese, milk, corn bread, and hot corn chips. Walter and Lawrence's mother Norah regularly buys milk and two pounds of ground beef from Charlie's store. Several people in their neighborhood have died in recent weeks, which Norah hates. Today it's Charlie. Last week it was Ann Turner, a local laundromat owner.

Charlie's body lies in the ditch, his mouth and eyes open.
A bloody sheet covers half of his naked body.

"They killed Ann," Norah had told her husband Thomas, who shook his head in disbelief. Norah, Thomas, Walter, Lawrence, and Fay, the baby, live in apartment 603 in one of high-rise projects. The hallway smells like urine because people frequently urinate there.

It had been different when Thomas and Norah first moved into the building. The halls were pristine. The floors were urine-free. Someone urinating on them would have made a person call someone's grandmother, and their grandmother would have made them clean it up. Back then, the mere sight of a chewed-up clump of gum on the hallway floor would have warranted a stern finger wagging. The neighborhood itself was not the best, but it was better than many. The people were not always the friendliest, but they looked out for one another. There was a common respect. A common decency. There were no discarded dead men in ditches. Back then, Norah and Thomas were young and happy and full of life. They married soon after meeting and then they had Walter. In time, Lawrence was born. Then Fay. They were happy. They laughed and loved in their small apartment.

Today Norah had let Walter and Lawrence walk home from school because Walter often asked to be allowed. In the past, Norah had always said "No."

"Norah, let the boys go," Thomas had said this morning.

Norah looked at the boys long and hard. "Yes, but go to school and come straight home," she told them.

When they got out of school, Walter said they were going to take a short cut home with his friend and classmate Earl, who also lives in their building.

"Why his lips always dry and peeling, like his Mama don't ever give him no grease?" Lawrence whispered to Walter about Earl as they walked from the school. Walter flicked Lawrence's head in response.

Earl gets off of his bike, puts it down, and climbs over it, still holding the handlebars. He walks over toward the ditch to get a closer look, picks up a rock, and throws it at Charlie. The rock bounces off Charlie's shoulder and lands on the grass. They all watch to see if he moves. He does not. The ditch is shallow, and if someone stands near the edge, they will fall in. Lawrence starts climbing down off the gate.

"I said stay right there! If you get up, I'm 'gone pop you upside your head," Walter yells.

Lawrence sits down.

"I wanna' see," Lawrence says. The other boys ignore him.

"I think he dead, too," Earl says, his half-smooched lint ball-filled hair is thick all over his head as if his mother does not comb it.

"Looks dead," Walter says, tilting his head to look at Charlie. His shoelaces are untied.

"Touch him," Earl says, scratching his face.

"I ain't touching him! You touch him!" Walter says.

"I *know* I ain't touchin' that man!" Lawrence says.

Walter quickly turns around and stares him down. "I ain't touching him!" Walter says again, this time as if he is mad.

Walter walks over, gets a stick, and starts poking Charlie; the freeze pop is swinging back and forth, hanging from his mouth between his teeth. He pokes Charlie's chest.

Earl watches closely. Walter takes the freeze pop out of his mouth, "Did he move?"

"Don't think so," Earl says, kneeling with his hands on his knees, his feet wide apart, to get a better look, balancing himself on the sides of his blue sneakers.

Walter hands Earl the stick, rubs his hand together, with all fingers spread out, and wipes them on his worn-out blue jeans, knees faded white and starting to tear.

Earl, his eyes bugged out, takes the stick and slowly pokes Charlie in his side. They stand still, waiting for him to move.

"Can I do it?" Lawrence asks Walter.

"Nope," Walter says, his eyes focused on Charlie.

"He dead; bet the police did it. My daddy say the police always killing black folks. Bet the police did this," Walter explains, walking up real close and looking into Charlie's stale wide-open eyes. Dark, dried and fresh, bright red blood are in the corners of his mouth. "Yeah, he dead."

"How you know?" Earl asks.

"Look at his eyes," Walter says pointing. "He dead and that's how stuff be looking when it be dead. He dead. Saw a dead bird and a dead cat. Once even saw a dead bullfrog in the middle of a road. His back half was crushed by a car. His mouth was open and eyes was looking *just* like that. All dead and gone. Glassy and full of tears that's about to fall but don't."

Earl puts his hands on the knees of his brown corduroy pants and looks real close, but is careful not to tilt over and fall on Charlie.

"He stink!" Walter says, frowning and fanning his nose. Earl frowns and nods, agreeing. Although he does not smell anything, Lawrence fans his nose too.

Earl gets on his bike and starts riding real slow, so slow that the pedals shake.

"Come on," Walter says. Lawrence grabs his book bag and runs to him. They walk beside Earl. Walter leans his head back and drinks the rest of his freeze pop, his shoelaces dragging behind him as he walks.

8003

Of all the police officers in Chicago, the department only sends two to the crime scene. Charlie's wife, Lana, was told that he was dead and ran out crying on Fourteenth Place without shoes, her hair undone and standing out like tired weeds all over her head.

"Lord, please help him!" she says, running through the crowd.

Lawrence watches from the kitchen window, sitting on Norah's lap, playing with her hand, holding his blue and white spin top.

Norah bought the blue and white spin top for Lawrence when they were at the grocery store together earlier in the day. There was candy inside of the package as well.

"You're eating that candy *too fast*," Norah said, as she watched Lawrence tear into the package, grab the candy, and stuff it into his mouth until his jaws protruded like a squirrel harboring nuts. Walter ate some of his candy very slowly and put the rest into his pocket. He has been eating it throughout the day.

"No," he said to Lawrence, when he asked if he could have some. Fay chewed on the corner of her unopened bag of candy. She put the plastic corner in her mouth and chewed very slow. Norah took it from her and put it on the top cabinet shelf beside a white box that's partially covered with brown, dried-up water stains. The box is filled with old plastic spoons and forks.

"Can I have some of Fay's candy, Momma?" Lawrence asked Norah

"No, sit on down and eat your own, boy," she said. Lawrence stood and looked at Fay's candy with his head held

10

back, and thought about the best ways he could climb the cabinet and get the candy.

Fay, wearing a pink shirt with a bird on it, now sits with her nose pressed against the kitchen window. Her hair is full of braids with pink barrettes on the tips that match her shirt. She has a dried-up jelly stain on her cheek.

"What are you looking at?" Norah says to Fay.

She puts Lawrence down and he drops his blue and white spin top. It rolls on its side across the floor. Norah walks over and looks at the crowd of people gathered beneath their window.

"What's going on out there?" she asks, looking down at the crowd. Lawrence sits on the floor under the table and tries to reach his spin top. He sees it under the radiator behind his mother's leg. Norah looks at Fay's face, gets a napkin, wets it, and wipes off the jelly stain. She looks out of the window again.

"I wonder what is going on," she says with her pinky finger in some dust that's in the corner of the brown, paint-chipped windowsill.

"Must have found Mr. Jackson," Walter says, looking down at a sheet of paper, doing his homework. He puts his pencil down. "Nineteen, twenty, twenty-one, twenty-two, twenty-three," he says counting on his fingers. He erases an answer and writes in a new one.

"Mama," Lawrence says, trying to reach past Norah's leg to get his top.

"What do you mean…they must have found Mr. Jackson?" Norah asks, her eyes wide open, and her head to the side.

"Someone killed him," Walter says, looking at his paper and writing. "Been in the ditch all day. Me, Lawrence, and Earl saw him hours ago," he says, writing with his head down.

"We *been* found him, Mama. The police be too late for stuff," he adds, curving his lips and scrunching his nose.

"What? Walter! Look at me!"

Walter looks at Norah, his fingers wrapped around his orange pencil tight. His eyes are big. His other hand is flat on the paper as if the wind is going to come through the window and blow it off the table.

"What...do...you...mean...you, Lawrence, and Earl found him?" Norah says with her eyes blinking mad. She's holding a blue and white worn-out checkered dishcloth, from which strings hang and water drips as she moves her hand.

"Someone killed him and threw him in the ditch. We found him. The police probably did it," Walter says as he starts slowly writing a crooked "49" on his paper, trying to make it straight.

"Mama," Lawrence says, looking up at Norah from under the table, wanting her to move so that he can retrieve his spin top. She does not move; rather she unknowingly stands in his way as he tries to reach the toy. Norah stares at Walter, her eyes wide and still.

"Mama!" Lawrence yells, looking up at her on his hands and knees.

Thomas walks in from work. Fay runs over to him, wobbling as if she is about to fall. He grabs her and picks her up.

"Why are you just telling me this now?" Norah says to Walter. "And my baby was out there, too. Did he see it?"

"I guess...Mr. Jackson was dead, Mama. His lips was all purple. I bet the police did it," Walter says again, shaking his head and looking at his homework. He puts the pencil's eraser on his lips and reads the next math problem.

"What happened?" Thomas asks.

"Charlie Jackson was killed. Walter, Lawrence, and Earl found him long before the police did, and Walter is just now telling me."

"What? Is that what all that mess is out there? Street full of people," Thomas says looking out of the window from across the room as he slowly puts Fay down, letting her feet drop to the floor. She reaches up for him to pick her up again, but he stretches his neck like an ostrich and looks toward the window.

"Yes. And Walter and Lawrence found him. And did not tell me anything. I see all those people out there," Norah says, pointing to the window, "and Walter says they were out there because of Charlie Jackson. Walter, you don't keep that stuff to yourself! You understand me? You tell me when you see stuff like that!"

"Where was he, Walter?" Thomas asks.-

"In the ditch. Dead. Somebody killed him," Walter says.

"What did you and Lawrence do?"

"I made Lawrence sit on the gate. Then Earl and me poked Charlie with a stick. Then we all went to the store. Earl bought a juice 'cause his Mama gave him a quarter this morning. I brought Lawrence and me some bags of chips. Hot ones. Didn't have enough for juice and chips because I was seven cents short."

"You could have gotten yourself and your brother hurt out there, Walter!" Norah says. "Did you touch him?"

"Noooooooooo," he says shaking his head. "I wasn't touchin' him. He was dead, Mama. And he was stinkin'," he adds, frowning and writing.

Thomas walks to the window and looks out. He is wearing his work uniform and worn-out steel-toe boots. The steel part is partially showing through the ripped and worn leather.

Charlie Jackson's body is still in the ditch with the white sheet covering it. There is yellow tape around the crime scene. The two cops walk around the body as if they are busy working, but they are not. They look at their watches and write on their note pads. Hundreds of people stand around and attempt to look at Charlie and gossip about who they think did it. They stand, try to look past the police, frown hard, and whisper in each other's ears. Then they stand with their noses turned up and their arms crossed, as if they had solved the murder.

Thomas shakes his head, his hands deep in his pockets fidgeting with his keys, which jangle and bang against coins.

Outside, Lana tries to run through the police tape, but a man grabs her. She falls to her knees, screaming. The man holds her around her waist in order to restrain her.

Norah shifts a little. Lawrence reaches for his spin top. Norah quickly picks him up so that he does not burn his hand on the radiator.

A Needed Change

"We have to get out of here, Thomas. This is too much," Norah says, tying her scarf on her head and looking in the bathroom mirror, preparing for bed. It is 10:34 pm. She turns around and looks at Thomas, who sits on the bathtub without a shirt, wearing brown slacks which are unbutton, his bare feet pressed against the white and black linoleum floor. "The kids didn't need to see that…and Walter did not tell us…did not say one thing…like it was nothing," she continues.

"They've seen stuff like that before," Thomas says.

She turns to him and looks him in his eyes. "Theyain'tneverseenadeadbody! They don't need to see that! We have to get these kids out of here!" He looks at her tired face, her frown lines growing deeper and dark circles forming around her bulging eyes. He stands up, hugs her tight, and rubs the back of her head. Then he closes his eyes and rests his head on hers.

"That's what you want?" he says rubbing her shoulder. She nods. They both stand silent. "Then we'll get out of here. I'm going to do everything in my power to get us out of here," he says, his eyes still closed as he slowly sways with her.

Norah smiles and wraps her arms around his bare waist, his body slim and muscular; his skin, a deep hickory, is warm, sweaty, and soft.

"We'll get out of here, OK?" He looks down at her round face and small eyes, her short and heavy frame. "OK, Baby?" he asks. She nods with her head deep in his chest. He kisses her scarfed head.

Peanut Butter and Jelly

"Boy, get down from there!" Thomas yells.

Walter is standing on the kitchen table, holding an open loaf of white bread. The bread bag swings in one hand. The red twist tie is in his other. Thomas stares him down.

"What are you doing up there?"

Walter looks at his father and does not say a word, his eyes wide and sweat forming on his forehead. "Get down!" Thomas says again, blinking and struggling to adjust his eyes to the light. He stands there in his tan pajamas. He was on his way to the bathroom but stopped when he saw Walter.

"What are you doing up there?"

"Making a peanut butter and jelly sandwich," Walter says, his voice low and soft, nervously trawling the twist tie between his fingers. "Peanut butter up there," he says, pointing to the wooden cabinet above the kitchen table.

"You gone hurt yourself. It's 2:38am in the morning," Thomas says, looking at the clock hanging near the sink. "Come here." Walter walks across the table barefoot and stands there, his toes trembling as they peer over the table's edge. Thomas lifts him down.

"What if you would have hurt yourself?" Thomas asks. Walter stands silently, looking at the wooden cabinet, then the floor.

Thomas stares at him. Walter stands there in his dark-blue airplane pajamas and a light blue robe, which is oversized and hangs off of him.

"Didn't your Mama cook y'all dinner?"

Walter nods.

"But you still hungry?"

Walter looks down.

Thomas walks to the cabinet, takes out the peanut butter, and places it on the table.

"Get two plates," he says, his voice strained and hoarse.

"OK," Walter says and gets two plates. Thomas places two slices of bread on each of them, then takes the jelly out of the refrigerator and places it on the table.

"Which one do you want to spread? Peanut butter or jelly?"

"Jelly."

"OK." He opens the jar of jelly and sets it in front of Walter. "I'll do the peanut butter." Thomas opens the jar of peanut butter, his huge knuckles around the cap. Walter slowly spreads jelly on two slices of bread and Thomas slowly spreads peanut butter on two slices of bread.

Walter picks up a wooden chair, but can barely carry it to the table. Thomas helps him. They pass each other a slice of bread and press it down on the other.

"You scared your mother today," Thomas says.

"I did," Walter says and tilts his head to the side as he slowly sits in the chair.

"Yep. I need you to tell us when you see stuff like that, OK?"

"OK."

Walter reaches over and presses down on Thomas's sandwich, his dark brown fingers spread out as he presses gently to ensure that the peanut butter and jelly are well mixed. Thomas watches, silent.

"We are going to move out of here," Thomas says

"Where we moving to?"

"Not sure yet, but a place safer than this."

They both sit silent. Both look at the sandwiches on their tan glass plates. Thomas's plate is chipped on the left side.

"Bet the police did it," Walter says.

"Bet the police did it, too," Thomas says with a smirk on his face. Walter smiles and nods.

They pick up their sandwiches and take bites as they sit side-by-side in the dim kitchen, chewing and giggling.

Sky Diving

Norah sits on a concrete bench in the small neighborhood playground, holding Fay on her lap. Thomas sits beside them, wearing his brown work uniform and work boots. Nearby, Walter pushes Lawrence on a swing. Both are dressed in huge fall jackets. Walter's is blue and Lawrence's is red and black.

"So, what do we do now?" Norah asks, her hands around Fay's waist.

Thomas shakes his head. His eyes are low, yellowish, and filled with red veins. He takes off his hat and clenches it so tight that his brown fingers turn red.

"Faster!" Lawrence yells. Walter pushes harder.

Thomas looks at the ground, focusing on the brown and yellow leaves, trembling with the breeze.

"We'll get through this, Thomas," Norah says and rubs his hand; his brown work gloves laying on his thigh shake as he slightly moves. He looks at her hand and takes it into his.

"You'll get another job. You always do," she says. "We've been through hard times before. This is just another thing that we'll get through. OK? We'll live on beans and rice if we have to."

"We have to postpone moving until I find something else," he says, biting his top lip, digging his teeth into the flesh.

"I know," she whispers. She touches his face; his chin is hard and broken with lines, his scruffy beard is graying.

He slouches on the bench and looks around. Some distance away, a young man is selling drugs to an older man, drug addicts and alcoholics sit and stand and walk in a daze, and a group of teens stand on the street corner. Thomas wipes his forehead and stares at the line of liquor stores, abandoned boarded-up buildings, and deserted store fronts that used to be shops and restaurants.

"I'll get us out of here in time," he says, tears forming in the corners of his eyes. Norah closes hers and nods.

"Faster!" Lawrence yells again. Walter pushes harder.

Walter gives Lawrence a big push. When the swing is high in the air, Lawrence jumps out, afraid. He soars into the air and lands on his hands and knees, his fingertips deep in the gravel and leaves.

"Lawrence!" Norah yells. Norah and Thomas quickly jump up and run to Lawrence. Norah carries Fay, whose arms and legs swing in a pink jacket and pink corduroy pants. Lawrence cries and the tears runs down his face. "Lawrence!" Norah says, breathing heavy, her eyes big.

"*Boy*, get up!" Thomas yells as he pulls Lawrence up by his arm. "Why did you let him do that, Walter? A man looks after his family. You need to look after him."

Walter stands in disbelief and looks into his father's eyes. Then he looks at Lawrence, whose tears run from his eyes, down his cheeks, and onto the gravel and colorful, dirty leaves.

"Lawrence, why did you do that?" Norah asks, shaking, as Thomas brushes him off. "Don't do that again!" Lawrence stands in the middle of the gravel and the leaves, bleeding from a cut on his hand. The blood runs down his fingers and thumb.

Walter, his black cap crooked on his head, stands as if in a trance with his eyes wide and his mouth slightly open, staring at Lawrence's hand. Norah shakes her head in disbelief, takes a tissue out of her purse, and wipes at the cut. Fay stands wobbling beside her, holding her pants leg and trying not to fall. Thomas picks her up and places her under his arm as if she's a football.

"Hold his hand, Walter," Thomas says, shaking his head and breathing heavy. Lawrence cries softly, his cut hand snuggled in Walter's pocket, clutched tight.

₧₧

"Don't do that anymore," Walter says, holding Lawrence's hand. They are at home in their small bathroom. Lawrence, silent, looks at Walter, frowning. "Mama say put some of this on it," Walter says, holding a bottle of rubbing alcohol.

Lawrence snatches his hand away. "That's gone burn," he says, looking at the bottle of alcohol and holding his wounded hand behind his back in a balled fist.

"You have to be a big boy and let me put this on you. Come on," Walter says and reaches for Lawrence's hand.

"No! It's gone burn!" Lawrence pulls his hand away again, still looking at the bottle of alcohol. Tears roll down his face and mucus slides from his nose. His chubby stomach is poking out from underneath his long-sleeved green shirt and hanging over the rim of his hand-me-down blue jeans, the pant legs rolled up to his ankles. Walter reaches into his pocket and takes out a plastic toy bubble. In it is a little green car. He brought it from a laundromat vending machine when he and Norah did the laundry.

"I will give you this if you be a big boy and let me put this on you," he says and shows Lawrence the bubble toy with the car inside. Lawrence stares at the toy with his mouth open and eyes sparkling. "You want it? OK, Mama say I have to put alcohol on your cut to kill the germs," he says, holding the bubble in his hand like it is a valuable treasured prize. Lawrence nods, tears still in his eyes. "OK, you can't cry. You just have to let me put it on you, ok?" Lawrence nods again. "OK, give me your hand…I have to wash it first, OK?"

They watch as the water runs over Lawrence's hand, washing the blood from the open wound and running down the drain.

Walter takes a huge yellow towel from the towel rack and dries Lawrence's hand thoroughly. Lawrence watches, silent, his eyes focused on the towel. Walter carefully pours some rubbing alcohol on a cotton ball and takes Lawrence's hand. Lawrence's eyes, big and watering up, stare at the cotton ball.

"Don't look at it!" Walter orders. "Look that way," he says, pointing to a spot in the corner of the bathroom, between the door and wall. Lawrence turns his head and looks into the corner.

"Like that and keep looking that way," Walter says.

"OK." Lawrence braces himself so hard that the veins protrude from his neck. He stands with his fingers spread out and hand shaking.

Walter quickly rubs the alcohol-soaked cotton ball on Lawrence's cut. Lawrence grimaces with his eyes closed and begins to cry.

"Here, here, here," Walter says and gives him the toy bubble. Lawrence takes it and looks at the green car inside, closely and carefully, as Walter places a bandage on the small cut. "Don't do that anymore, OK?" He looks into Lawrence 's eyes as he rubs the bandage to ensure that it doesn't fall off. "You could have killed yourself," he continues, tearing up. "I have to look after you better. Don't do that anymore, OK?" Walter stands, slightly taller than his brother. Lawrence nods.

"Open this," Lawrence says, giving Walter the bubble toy and wiping the tears from his face and the snot from his nose with the back of his hand. Walter opens the toy and hands Lawrence back the bubble and the green car.

"Mama and Daddy said we not moving yet, so we have to be more careful. You can't be doing crazy stuff like that, OK?" Walter says.

Lawrence nods and runs out of the bathroom, excited. He holds the green car in one hand and the snot-covered bubble in the other.

He moves the bottle away from her reach,
laughing and shaking his head...

Having a Party

Thomas is singing with his eyes closed. Sam Cooke's "Having a Party" blasts from the record player on the dresser.

Now Thomas is slowly dancing in the middle of the living room floor, holding a half-finished bottle of whiskey. The whiskey bottle's black top is on the end table, next to a dark green, leaf-shaped ashtray with a small, dingy-white chip on the side. There's a burned-out cigarette there. Thomas's white dress-shirt has the top buttons open; it's wrinkled and part of it is hanging out of his pants. Under his white wrinkled shirt, there's white T-shirt stained with bright yellow sweat. Thomas has been looking for a job for weeks, but has not yet found one.

"They keep telling me 'no,' so I need a drink when I come home," he said to Norah one night. Now every day when he comes home, he grabs a bottle and sits around with his head down, sucking his teeth and drinking. Thomas continues singing, but stops to take a sip from the whiskey bottle. The setting sunlight shines through the yellow curtain into the living room. Thomas sings, wearing an old brown beat-up wide-brimmed hat, his black, wrinkled tie loose around his neck. "Come on, Lawrence," he says, reaching out to his son.

Lawrence looks at his father and smiles. "Come on y'all, help Daddy," Thomas says. The children get up and start dancing with their father, trying not to fall. Thomas dances, staggering beside them. He had gotten up at 5:00am and was out all day. When he came home, he was holding a brown paper bag that was dirty from the cigarette stains on his hands, twisted tight, and shaped like a bottle. "Everybody dance now," Thomas says, taking a sip from his bottle and moving side to side.

"We dancing," Walter says, his eyes closed and face contorted as if he feels the music like his father does. Their Grandma says that Walter is tall, dark, and lean like Thomas. Lawrence is short, brown, and round like Norah. She describes Fay as light yellow. She had bent down and looked at Fay. "She came here not looking like nobody."

"Come on, kids!" Thomas says. Lawrence shakes and kicks his legs.

Thomas picks up Fay, who reaches for the whiskey bottle.

"You want some of this?" he says, holding the whiskey bottle out to her. "You can't have none of this." He moves the bottle away from her reach, laughing and shaking his head, his face full of sweat, rolling down his forehead, nose, and arm, and into the rolled-up sleeves of his wrinkled shirt. Whiskey is heavy on his hot breath. "Having a good time dancing to the music," he sings, rocking with Fay.

Norah walks into the living room and looks around. There is paper everywhere and the furniture is out of place. The music is so loud that the walls shake. Thomas is holding Fay and staggering with the whiskey bottle in his hand. The whiskey is now nearly finished. Walter and Lawrence are dancing beside him. Norah looks at him, her eyes like slits, her jaw puffed out. She walks over, turns the record player off, and takes the whiskey bottle out of Thomas's hand. She takes Fay from him and puts her on the floor. Then she takes Thomas's hand into hers and starts leading him toward their bedroom, holding him up so that he does not fall.

"No baby, we are having a party," Thomas says slowly, his eyes low and drooping. He wobbles back and forth and bumps into the corner of the couch.

Although the music is off, Walter continues dancing with Thomas. Fay and Lawrence are dancing as well. Fay mainly jumps and laughs in an attempt to do what the older children are doing. Lawrence holds her hands and moves with her from side to side. "Dancing to the music." Thomas closes his eyes and puts his hands in the air, his hat nearly falling off his head. Norah stands silent and looks at them all. She walks to the record player, turns it back on, then walks back to Thomas and wraps her arms around him.

She sings like she's Sam Cooke and rocks slowly with Thomas. He opens his red eyes and looks at her, smiles and kisses her, moving his hips from side to side.

"Take off his other shoe, Walter," Norah says as she removes Thomas's right shoe. Walter slowly unties the left one and takes it off. Thomas sits asleep on the couch, snoring loud with his arms folded and hands in his armpits. "Get your sister, Lawrence," Norah whispers as Fay starts to climb on top of Thomas, stepping on his stomach. He does not awaken. Norah takes off his tie and shirt, placing them on the arm of the couch to take into the bedroom with her later. "When he finds a job, he will feel better. Then we are moving." Norah had told the children before Thomas came home.

"Ready?" she now asks. Walter and Lawrence nod that they are ready. They pick up Thomas's legs, and push his lower body up as she pushes his upper body down onto the couch. Fay pushes, too, but Thomas does not move. Norah puts a blanket over him and turns off the light, holding his folded shirt and tie in her arms up to her chest. "Come on," she whispers. The children follow, leaving Thomas in the dark, snoring into his armpit and hand.

Another Day

"Norah!" Thomas yells from the living room. He has been searching for a job all night and has just returned.

Lawrence had stood by the window, waiting for him. Finally, his son spotted him, rained-soaked with his hands in his pocket. He quickly turned the corner and rushed toward their building's entrance. "Daddy!" Lawrence yelled from the window, but Thomas did not hear him.

"Lawrence, get out of that window," Norah had said.

"Norah!" Thomas now yells again from the living room. Norah walks in. Thomas sits on the couch, taking off his boots, hunched over.

"How'd it go?" Norah asks. "Did you find something?"

Thomas shrugs his shoulders, takes a wet, smashed pack of cigarettes out of his pocket and puts them on the end table along with a wrinkled newspaper with job listings circled in red pen and crossed out with a black one. He leans back, places his foot on his thigh, and scoots down. His face sags as if it is melting, his blood-clotted eyes are low.

"Are you hungry?" Norah asks, "I made stew and potatoes." He does not answer. He rubs his eyes and stares at his fingers. "We'll get through this, Thomas," Norah says. She puts his boots in the closet and closes the door.

Postponed

2:38a.m. Norah lies in bed alone. Thomas walks into their small dark bedroom. He takes off his hat and places it on their dresser. Then his watch. He places it beside his hat and a dim lit lamp. He takes off his slacks. Then he slowly unbuttons his shirt and takes it off. He folds his slacks and shirt and places them on a wooden chair beside their bed. He sits on their bed with his back to Norah. "I found a job," he says, his voice low. He pauses. "It's pretty far from here. Outside of Chicago." He looks at Norah, who looks him in his eyes. He looks away and faces the wall. Both are silent. "I will send you some money every two weeks for the kids." The dim light on the dresser illuminates their figures, their faces—the sweat on Thomas's forehead as it rolls to the tip of his nose and falls. "I'm going to move out there first...then I'll come back for y'all...then we gonna move outta here, Norah."

"Thomas, what are you saying to me?" Norah says, turning on her side.

"We moving, Norah. I found a job and we moving," he says.

"When?"

"A few weeks. A few months...when I get things worked out. I'm going down there first. Then I'm coming back for y'all...I'm going down there today."

"Today? Norah sits up. "Why you going today? Why can't we all go there together? Today? What you mean, *you going down there today?*"

"A buddy got something set up for me. I start Monday."

"What buddy?"

"A buddy."

"Who is this buddy? And why can't we all go down there, Thomas?"

"Norah, I just said I'm going down there first...then I'm coming back for y'all."

"Is this buddy a woman?"

"That ain't important."

"Ain't it?"

"I told you my plan."

"Why can't we go too? I can get these kids up and we can all get out of here."

Thomas shakes his head, "I gotta go first. You know...see how things are down there... then come back for y'all."

"How long is that gonna take?"

"Not, sure...." he says, looking around the room. "But you might have to start looking for a better job...you know... for the kids."

"I thought you said you was gonna send us some money?"

"I am, but I don't know for how long."

"Thomas, you make it sound like you ain't coming back"

"Naw....I'll be back...soon as I get on my feet. Don't know how long that's gonna take. Just give me some time."

"Thomas, don't do this to us," Norah says, her voice cracking and shaking and banging against her throat.

Thomas takes her hand in his. She pulls it away. He drops his head and places his hands on his knees. He sits without a shirt in blue boxers, his back to Norah.

"Thomas, what's going on? Can you just please tell me?"

"There ain't nothing here for me!"

"We here! What are you talking about?

He looks at her. "I know you are. You've always been. You a good woman. And we got some good kids."

"Thomas…"

"I just…I need to do this…for me."

"Do what?"

"Go down there."

"For how long?"

"I don't know."

Norah closes her eyes and clutches the pink and orange blanket to her chest, her hands shaking and warm from her racing blood.

She climbs out of the bed. The scarf on her head is tied with bow in the front. She is wearing a white, lace-trimmed nightgown and puts on a pink flowered robe that is missing a button. She bought the robe from the Goodwill store one Sunday after church, and realized that a button was missing when she got home. Now, her hands shake as she struggles with the remaining buttons and ties her robe. She walks into the kitchen. Thomas sits on the side of their bed in his blue boxer shorts, his hands firmly positioned on his knees, his bare feet firmly pressed against the floor.

₧₨

Norah stands beside the kitchen sink, holding it tight for fear that she might fall. She stares, in a daze, at the wooden cabinet. The only source of light is that of the street light peering in through the small kitchen window. The rest of the house is dark. The faucet, which has rust around the edges and knobs, slowly drips. Norah walks into the dark living room and sits on the sofa. The sound of the dripping faucet is accompanied by that of drawers opening and closing and metal hangers screeching against metal poles. Footsteps. Norah closes her eyes and focuses on the sound of the dripping water. The bedroom is again silent. Now, she feels Thomas's presence in the doorway. Although the living room is dark, she knows he is fully dressed and wearing his wool coat, insulated boots, hat, and gloves, and is holding a suitcase. Both are silent.

"I can't raise them by myself—I need you to help me raise them. I need you to help me. Please, Thomas," she says, her voice soft and trembling. Tears run down her lips, chin, and onto her white, lace-trimmed nightgown and pink flowered robe that has a missing button.

"Thomas," she says.

His suitcase brushes the closing door.

A Bag of Chips

"Momma! Can you take me to the store?" Lawrence asks, sitting on the kitchen floor, flicking a spoon around as if it's a toy. The spoon fell when Norah began washing the dishes. Norah stands in front of the sink, scrubbing a black pot with a steel pad. She looks down at him.

"Why do you want to go to the store?" asks Norah, submerging the pot in the greasy, soapy dish water and scrubbing it again. As she scrubs, sweat runs down her neck and water splashes on her white blouse.

"To buy some chips," Lawrence explains. "So, can we go?"

"No, because I just bought you some chips yesterday," she says.

"Can Daddy take me?"

Norah puts the pot, with a burnt spot still at the bottom, into the dish water and wipes her hands on her blue jeans, something she always tells the children not to do.

"Lawrence, get up."

Lawrence gets up and looks at her, still holding the spoon. She takes the spoon out of his hand and puts it in the greasy dish water. "I want you all to sit on the couch with Mama…

Walter, bring Fay." Walter takes Fay's hand and guides her to the couch. He picks her up, puts her down on the couch, and sits beside her. Lawrence walks over and sits down, his hands behind his back. Lawrence and Walter both look at Norah. "Daddy doesn't live with us anymore," Norah says.

Walter nods as if he is aware that his father has left.

"OK?" Norah says, looking at the children.

"Where Daddy at?" Lawrence asks. The whites of his eyes are showing almost fully.

"He just doesn't live with us anymore," Norah says.

Lawrence looks at Norah and places his hand between the couch's cushions, because he does not know what to do with it. One by one, he pulls items from underneath the cushion: a penny, a receipt, a bright pink barrette, a blue crayon, a ketchup packet. He places the items on the side table. Norah looks at him.

"Y'all put on your shoes and coats so we can go to the store," she says. Lawrence smiles, pulls his hand from underneath the couch cushion, and runs to his bedroom to put on his shoes.

Earline

"Ain't Miz Earline crazy?" Lawrence asks when they first spot Earline turning the corner as they walk down the street.

Norah grabs the children's hands, her grocery cart, and starts walking fast. "Come on y'all… Earline's coming." She pulls them up the street in the opposite direction with each swift step.

But Earline quickens her step and rushes up the street, trying to catch up to them. Norah looks back. She and the children begin running.

" Norah!" Earline calls.

At first, Norah acts as if she did not hear her.

"Norah! is that you?" Earline calls, hot on their tail. Still they run. "Norah!" Earline calls out, louder and louder. Running is no use, so Norah and the children stop.

"So, Norah, how are you?" Earline asks, standing before them now.

"Fine, Earline, how are you?" Norah answers.

"Fine," Earline says, then looks at Norah and the children. "It's just that I have not seen you in a while." She is holding tightly onto a white purse and wearing a black church hat and flowered dress. She's waiting for Norah to tell her business, because she feels that it is her right to know everything about everyone. "How is Thomas?" she asks and touches Norah's arm with the tips of her fingers, aware that Thomas has left. Everyone knows they were trying to move when Thomas left.

Norah smiles. She stands holding the handle of their metal grocery cart full of groceries. The bottom of the cart is bent because it once doubled as a stroller for Lawrence. Earline, her eyes wide, stares at Norah.

"How is he?" she asks again. She leans in a little with her arms folded, turns her head to the side, and squints. "See, Dolorous told me that you and Thomas broke up. I told her… that was not the truth!" Earline presses her lips tight.

"It was nice seeing you, Earline," Norah says. "Come on y'all," she says, taking Fay's hand. Lawrence puts his hand on the handle of the grocery cart. A spotted banana is on top, sticking up from one of the bags. They start walking. Walter walks beside them, holding a brown paper bag full of groceries in his arms. A carton of orange juice and a box of cereal sticks up from the top of the bag, which he holds so tight that it bends and starts to tear on the side. They all walk across the street, leaving Earline standing with her arms folded, still waiting for Norah's answer.

₧₧

When they get home, Norah walks into her bedroom and sits on her bed. She grabs the sides of her red blouse, pulls it over her head, and stares at a white coffee cup that is on the bedroom dresser. Beside the cup is the lamp and her black Bible, which has a missing cover; some of its pages are wrinkled and loose, tucked inside of it. Beside the Bible are a spool of red thread, a needle, a yellow opened envelope, and three safety pins. Norah sits in a daze, wearing a black, faded, stretched-out bra, her shoulders hunched over, her red blouse hanging from her wrist and touching the floor.

ಐCಐ

When they get home, Walter takes Fay's big pink and white coat off of her and puts it on the couch. He tries to help Lawrence take off his coat as well, but Lawrence tells him, "It's broke."

"Hold still," says Walter, holding the zipper in his hands, trying to work a small piece of the coat's fabric out of it. "Now, hold your head back'"

He's on his knees in front of Lawrence, who holds his head back so his chin does not get snagged in the zipper. Once Norah zipped it up and snagged his chin. He fell to the floor screaming and hollering. "I'm gone die," he had yelled, rolling around and kicking his legs.

"You got it?" he now asks his brother, looking at the ceiling, sweating, his lips dry.

"Yep," Walter says and zips Lawrence's coat up and down again. Fay sits in front of the dark television and watches it as if it is on. She sits, looking at it closely. Walter stands on a chair, puts their coats on hangers, and hangs them in the living room closet. Lawrence turns the television on and sits down next to Fay. She looks at him, then at the television, her eyes shining.

Now Walter folds the metal grocery cart and puts it into the pantry. Then he takes the groceries out of the bags and starts putting them away.

"Lawrence, turn the TV down a little, Mama's taking a nap," he whispers, putting a carton of eggs and a pound of ground beef into the refrigerator. Cereal, greens, spotted bananas, cornmeal, apples, tomatoes, bread, butter, fish, and a carton of orange juice sit on the table beside the bunch of wrinkled grocery store plastic bags and some big brown paper bags.

"OK," Lawrence whispers and turns the television down slowly, careful that he does not wake his mother.

Come Morning

Norah lies in bed perfectly still and looks at the ceiling.
Tears rest in her eyes, roll down the side of her face and onto
her pillow. She rises up and, with her head hung down, sits
on the edge of her bed and places her feet in her plush white
slippers.

Fay is laying on her back on the floor, playing with her
toy doll at the entrance to Norah's bedroom. Norah, eyes red,
looks at her.

"Fay," she whispers. Fay gets up and walks to her, her doll
underneath her arm.

"Who's that?" Noah says as she points to the doll, her
voice hoarse, "Can Mama see her?"

Fay looks at her doll. Norah, gently takes it into her hands
and looks at it closely. The doll is cotton with long, black yarn
hair. Her complexion is caramel. Her lips are red and smiling.
She has big, black eyes. Red shoes. And white socks.

There ain't nothing here for me: Thomas's words echo in
Norah's mind. As she plays with her daughter, her tears fall
on the doll. Fay watches. Norah looks at her and rubs the dolls
hair. "Where are your brothers?" Norah asks. Fay returns her

mother's glance and touches the doll's hair. "Boys, come here! Walter! Lawrence!" Norah tries to say this forcefully, but her voice is strained and low as if it slipped from her and fell to the floor at her feet.

Walter walks into the bedroom, almost completely dressed. He holds a blue sweater in his hand.

"Yes, Mama?" he says, sitting next to her on the bed. He's wearing blue pants and a blue shirt and black shoes. He has so much grease in his hair that it shines—he's dressed both himself and Lawrence. With his head down, he slides his feet from side to side against the floor.

Lawrence wipes his eyes with the back of his hand as he walks into the bedroom, stands in front of Norah and places his hand on her knee. Norah looks at her children: Fay, trying to take the attached shoe off of her doll; Walter, sliding his feet from side to side; and Lawrence, fully dressed, now yawning, one hand on her knee and the other picking at the corner of his eye.

"What do you all want for breakfast?" she asks, her heart pulling in her chest. Hot. Her un-scarfed, tangled hair droops like shriveled weeds bruised and beaten by the sun and heavy rain. She has tears in her baggy eyes, with wrinkles underneath and dried-up tear blotches on her cheeks.

"I'll fix breakfast, Mama," Walter says.

She looks at him and touches his face. "No, I'll make breakfast. Can you set the table for Mama?" she asks Lawrence.

Lawrence runs out of the room. Fay picks up her doll and follows, trying to keep up. Walter looks up at Norah with tears in his own eyes and wipes her eyes with his hand. He hugs her, his eyes closed, his shiny afro brushing against her chin.

"Come on, help your Mama up," Norah says. Walter puts his sweater down beside him and gently holds Norah's forearm and elbow as she lifts herself from her bed. They slowly walk into the kitchen. Walter's arm is around Norah's waist tight, trying to hold her up. She walks a little, pauses, rest herself on the door frame, and tries again, Walter is at her side, gently guiding her steps.

⁊ᑍᑕ⳼

The smell of eggs, bacon, and oatmeal spill through the kitchen. As Norah cooks breakfast, she watches Walter comb Fay's hair, her head tilting with each stroke from a blue comb.

"Hold still," Walter says, "Let me see." He steps back and looks at her hair from a distance, trying to see if both sides are even. "You have to hold still," he says as he walks back, and then carefully parts her hair. He holds a lock of hair between his fingers and braids it, holding the comb in his mouth. An open jar of grease is on the couch inches away from them, its black top to the side of it. Rubber bands, barrettes, and bobby pins are in a faded, white plastic butter bowl beside the open jar of grease and its black top.

Lawrence lies on the floor on his stomach, one leg kicked up on a stool, drinking a strawberry juice box and watching morning cartoons.

Norah looks at them all, takes a deep breath, and stirs the oatmeal. The bacon and eggs sizzle in the frying pan.

45

Ain't Got Here Yet

"Mama's looking for a job," Lawrence says, sitting at his grandparent's kitchen table, staring at his food.

Walter looks up at him and shakes his head. "I know that already."

Their grandfather had picked them up from school.

"She supposed to come get us, but she ain't got here yet," Lawrence adds.

"Stop talking to me," Walter says.

Norah has been looking for another job for some time, but still has not found one. Now the children's grandfather sits in his chair, asleep with his mouth open. Lawrence stands over him, looking into his mouth, waiting for his mother.

"She ain't got here yet. Called and said she was coming, but she ain't got here yet," Lawrence says again. Walter ignores him and eats his dinner as if Lawrence had not said a word.

Fay is asleep in their grandparents' room. Now, their grandmother comes out of the bedroom with big pink rollers on one side of her hair. The other side is freshly curled and shiny. The soft smell of oil sheen floats about her like a cloud.

"Lawrence, are you done with your food?" She walks to the kitchen table and looks at Lawrence's plate. His steak and potatoes are gone, but his baby carrots are still there.

"Lawrence, eat these carrots!" she says. He walks to the table, sits down, and looks at his hands, his jaws puffed.

"Your Mama will be here soon, so when you are both done eating, get your things together. She'll be here any minute," their grandmother says.

"OK, Grandma," Walter says, eating, holding his fork tight, his mouth open and chewing wide, his head so low to his plate that his chin almost touches his food.

Their grandmother walks back into the bedroom, taking a roller out of her hair.

Lawrence walks over to his grandfather and looks into his gaping mouth again. His grandfather sits there with his head leaning back against the chair, snoring hard. Lawrence drops a carrot in his mouth. His grandfather makes a sound as if he choking, jumps up, and spits the carrot out into his hand. He looks at it closely to determine what it is. Then, he looks at Lawrence, his eyes wide and full of fire. He takes off his belt.

Just then, someone knocks on the door. Lawrence runs to it, hoping it's his mother . He opens it and Norah is standing there, looking at him. She walks in and Lawrence runs behind her, grabbing her coat.

"Get over here!" yells her father at Lawrence. He's nearly stumbling and falling as he holds the belt and tries to catch Lawrence.

"Daddy, what he'd do?" Norah asks looking around, almost out of breath.

"What's going on?" their grandmother says, rushing out of the bedroom. She's taken out another roller and the pink spongy part of it falls off and rolls beside a couch leg. Her bare feet slap against the floor, loud.

Their grandfather sits back down in the chair, still holding his belt in his hand.

"What did you do?" Norah asks, looking down at Lawrence.

"I gave Granddad one of my carrots because I can't eat them all by myself," he says, swinging the front of her coat and looking up at her.

Their grandfather leans back, shakes his head, and closes his eyes, his legs crossed and hands folded on his stomach.

In a Moment

"I'm coming, Walter," Norah says. Walter holds the elevator door open for her. She quickly rushes through the door, holding a bag of groceries and unzipping her purse for her keys. The elevator goes up; the door opens.

"Thomas!" Norah says. Thomas stands outside of their door at the end of the hallway, looking at them.

"Daddy!" Lawrence screams and runs to his father. Norah stands, holding Fay's hand. Walter stands beside them.

"I was hoping ya'll still lived here," Thomas says and walks toward them. Norah looks at him. Into his eyes. He looks down. Then up again. He stares at Walter, who holds his stare then takes his mother's hand. He then looks at Fay. Norah opens the door. She, Walter, Lawrence, and Fay walk into the apartment, then away from the opened door. Thomas walks in, closes the door, and looks around. Most of the furniture is the same and in its original place. Norah puts the bag of groceries on the kitchen table. She takes off her coat and hangs it up. Walter takes off his coat and helps Lawrence and Fay out of theirs. He hangs them all up. Norah takes a carton of milk out of the brown paper bag and puts it into the refrigerator. Thomas, silent, stands by the door. He takes a napkin out of his pocket and wipes his mouth, staring at Norah, who sits in a brown chair that is beside the kitchen window. She looks at Thomas, who now watches Walter as he takes the remaining items out of the grocery bag: a bag of apples, a carton of orange juice, butter, and a bag of corn meal. Walter takes Lawrence and Fay by their hands and guides them into a bedroom.

"Thomas, what are you doing here? Norah says with her hands pressed into her thighs, her knuckles resting on her newly formed rolls.

"I wanted to see you and the kids," Thomas says, his hands in his pocket and his coat under his arm.

"For what?"

"Y'all been on my mind." He touches the arm of a chair and looks at it, then back at Norah. "I'm sorry, Norah."

"Thomas, don't come in here after disappearing for months and tell me you're sorry."

He looks down.

"But I am, Norah. I should have ended things better," he says, his voice soft and low.

"*Why* are you *here*?"

"I feel it's time to be here. Time to explain to you why I left. I was going through some things and didn't know how to handle it…. Losing my job and you wanting to move. I was under so much pressure."

"I was, too."

"I know…I know. I made a mistake. I should not have left."

"Did she put you out? Is that it?"

He looks at her, licks his lips, and stares at his shoes.

"Is it?" Norah says.

"It ain't about her," Thomas says.

"The hell it ain't!"

"I'm trying to talk to you. What's done is done, but I'm here now."

"Thomas, these are your kids and you can see them any time you want. You don't need me to tell you that."

"Norah, you can't raise these kids by yourself. You, need me here to help you."

"You don't have to be here to help me."

"But I want to be. I'm home, Norah."

"You can see the kids any time you want."

"Can I see you?"

Norah gets up, puts water in the burnt pot, places it on the stove, and lights the burner. She takes a piece of catfish out of the refrigerator, washes it, and places it on a platter. Her back is to him. He watches her, wringing his brown skullcap in his hands. He has sweat on his brow, which rests and runs down the bridge of his nose. He rubs his eyes, puts on his hat, and leaves as Norah pours corn meal on the fish, covering it completely.

The Hall

"Just sit right here. Walter, please watch them," Norah says. The children sit in black plastic chairs in a long hallway that has blue-carpeted floors and white walls inside of a posh downtown building. Norah's hair is pined into a ponytail and she is wearing a dress shirt, a black skirt, a blazer, and black dress shoes for a job interview. She brought the children with her because she could not find a babysitter. Earlier she took out their winter clothing and wrapped them up. "Got to get this good and tight, so the Hawk won't get you," she said, as she tied Lawrence's scarf.

"The Hawk?" Lawrence turned around quickly, asking, "What's that?"

"Yeah, what's the Hawk, Momma?" Walter said.

"The blood-chilling wind out there is called the Hawk. It's cold, quick, and hunts in Chicago. We've got to wrap up so it won't get us."

"Oooh, Momma! The Hawk be hitting people in the face real hard. One time, I could not even feel my face it was so cold. 'The Hawk' got me. He whacked me in the face and almost knocked me down. You had to hold me Momma because I was going to go flying across the street."

"I remember that," Norah said, and smiled. "See, that's why we have to warp up. OK?" Lawrence and Walter nodded.

Now they sit in the hallway as Norah puts Lawrence's blue and gray gloves together and rolls them into a ball. They came here on a bus in the snow. "The big mean green," Norah said, describing the CTA bus to the children. "Always late and even later when it's cold. Especially when there's snow on the ground. It's extremely late then. Too late," she said.

"Wait right here," Norah said to the children as they stood at the bus stop. "Hold their hands, Walter." Walter grabbed one each of Lawrence's and Fay's hands and held them tight. Norah stepped into the street and searched the distance for an approaching bus. She stood looking down the street and rubbing her hands together, shaking with the cold. The children were shaking too, even Fay.

"It's the Hawk," Lawrence said, his voice horse.

Walter nodded. The ground, streets, houses, cars, tree branches, everything around them was covered in snow.

"Nope," Norah had said, walking back to the sidewalk. As she spoke, some of her body heat, like a tiny white cloudy ball, bounced off her lips and escaped into the air.

They waited for some time before the bus came. When it came, they were so cold that their noses were running and their eyes were full of frozen tear drops. They boarded quickly. Walter and Lawrence ran to two seats that were next to the window. Lawrence was on his knees looking out of the window. He pulled his scarf down from his face, so that he could see, and wiped the window with his glove. Norah stood at the front, paying the bus driver their fares. The bus driver looked at his watch, punched the time on her transfer, and gave it back to her.

"Lawrence, sit down right," Norah said to him, as she sat beside him. He stretched his legs out in front of himself and sat correctly in his seat. Norah held Fay on her lap.

Now, Norah stands beside the black plastic chairs in the hallway, making sure they did not drop any of their things on the floor. She takes off Fay's gloves and puts them into a bag. She then takes some tissue out of her purse and wipes Fay's face. Lawrence holds on to the pole of a floor lamp that is to the side of him and slides down his chair to the floor.

"Lawrence, get up!" Norah says. "Get … up!" She picks him up by his arm and sits him back down in the chair. "Listen to your brother," she says, wagging her finger at him. All of their coats are on a chair beside them in a huge pile. About five plastic grocery bags are on the floor, with extra clothing and food inside of them. Some bags are doubled because there are holes in them. Three of the bags are tan, two are white, and all have the names of stores on them. Walter pulls the bags over by him and puts them between his big black and blue boots. Lawrence's boots are blue and gray. Fay's are pink and white. "I will be out soon," Norah says.

"OK, Momma," Walter says, looking up at her, still trying to ensure with his foot that all of the bags are between his boots.

Norah walks over to Lawrence and kneels down. "Stand up for Momma." He stands up in front of her. She starts fixing his sweater, then wipes his hair and pats it down, careful not to mess up his part. "Lawrence, I want you to listen to your brother, OK?"

He nods as he rolls his tongue against his jaw, reaches back and touches his chair, which has a bumpy seat. Norah takes his chin in her cold hand. "Lawrence, do what he says, OK?" He nods, sits down, and rubs his hands on his chair, smacking his seat. Norah picks up her purse and walks down the long hallway into an open office. Lawrence slides down his chair, holding the lamp pole.

∓

"You want this one?" Walter asks, pulling an apple cereal bar from one of the plastic bags.

"No," Lawrence says and looks into the bag. Walter takes out a strawberry bar and an apple bar and holds them up to Fay. She takes the strawberry one out of his hand, but she does not know the difference. She just takes it because it is closest to her. Walter opens it for her and gives it back. Lawrence takes another strawberry one out of the box that's inside of one of the plastic bags and gives it to Walter to open for him. Walter opens it and gives it back to Lawrence. Norah had told them that they could eat the cereal bars if they were hungry.

Walter starts re-packing the remaining bars and placing them into a bag. Lawrence sees an open door down the hall. He walks over to it and stands in the doorway, eating his cereal bar. A white man sitting at a desk, writing, looks up at him. Walter walks over, grabs Lawrence's hand, takes him back to his chair, and sits him down. Lawrence hits Walter on his arm. Fay gets up from her chair. Walter picks her up and puts her on his lap. She almost falls, but he holds her tight around her waist.

"You want another one?" he asks, holding another cereal bar up to her, which he dug out of the plastic bag, which has crumbs at the bottom. She nods, although her first one is still unfinished.

"Where the juice?" Lawrence asks.

"In one of the white plastic bags," Walter says.

Lawrence bends down, gets a juice out of one of the white plastic bag, and opens it. The white man that was sitting at the desk in the office now stands in the doorway and looks at them. He is chubby. A patch of thick brown curly side hair partially circles a bold spot. A few strings fight to make their way to the other side of his hairline, but get stuck in the middle. He is wearing a white shirt with the sleeves rolled up to his elbows, and a loose black tie. He has a wide face that curves and twists like a bull dog. He stands and stares at them with his eyes low, his bushy eyebrows twitching, and his mouth moving as if he is mumbling or chewing on his tongue.

Walter opens a juice box and gives it to Fay.

"What are y'all doing out here?" the man asks with his hands in his pockets, his brown pants legs flooding, revealing his black socks.

"Waiting on our Momma," Walter says. "She down there." He points down the hall to the other office. The white man looks down the hall and back at the children. Walter stares at him hard, locking eyes with him. Lawrence gets up.

"Sit down, Lawrence!" Walter says, his eyes still locked on the white man. Lawrence sits down. The white man nods at Walter, walks back into his office, and closes the door.

Norah hurriedly walks down the hallway, smiling. "OK, come on." She takes Fay's coat from the chair and starts putting it on her. Walter and Lawrence start putting on theirs. It's the third time they've done this routine this week. Walter and Lawrence put on their hats and gloves and Norah ties their scarves tight around their faces.

Walter pulls his scarf away from his mouth. "What happened?" he asks, his black skullcap covering his eyebrows.

"I start next Wednesday," Norah says, smiling.

Walter's eyes widen. "So, we gonna move soon?"

"Yep," Norah says, still smiling. Walter smiles back and puts his scarf over his mouth. They all go outside and battle the Hawk, walking fast with their scarves tied tight over their mouths, pushing through the snow.

A New Day

"It is not the best, but it is better," Norah says to Walter, Lawrence, and Fay. They stand staring at a two-story brownstone apartment building, where they will now live. The building is on a quiet street in a peaceful neighborhood where crime, although present, is not as high as where they came from. The streets are lined with nice houses and brownstone apartment buildings with freshly mowed lawns, elaborate flower beds, shrubs, and hedges. There are trimmed trees that line the walkways. Movers are carrying boxes from the van into the brownstone apartment building.

"This our new house Mama," Lawrence says, looking up at the building.

"It's our new apartment," Norah says, with tears in her eyes.

"Why it's not as big as the other one we use to live in? The other one went way, way high," he says, demonstrating with his hands, elevating them.

"Because this is not a project," Walter says, looking at Lawrence. "The other building was a project. Right, Mama?"

"It was, but it severed us while it did," she says.

"Momma, did we move because the police was going to kill us like they killed Charlie?" Lawrence asks, squinting, his finger up to lips, his jaw puffed.

"No, the police did not kill Charlie," Norah says.

"I bet they did, Momma. They be killing black people," Walter says, nodding.

"Some do, but Charlie was not killed by the police. Charlie died because some people wanted his store and he did not want to sell it. There was a lot money being made on that little corner. The police found the people who did it and arrested them. Lina was behind it. They arrested her, too. They also killed Ann. Everybody knew that laundromat was making money."

"Did they die because they were Black, Mama?" Walter asks.

"No, greed killed them. Greed doesn't care about race. It just kills. We moved because there was too much crime and I want you all to have better. Like I said, this isn't the best, but it's better. And when I go back to school and finish, we're gonna have even better."

Blinking rapidly, Lawrence and Walter up look at her. "OK?" she asks and takes a deep breath. They nod. She looks around and watches as the movers carry in the last few boxes. Fay pulls on Norah's coat. Norah picks her up. "What do you want?" Norah asks, smiling and looking into Fay's eyes. Fay smiles and puts her head on her mother's chest. Norah looks at the brownstone. "Let's go inside," she says.

"Me first!" Lawrence says.

"Walter, hold the door!" Norah says. Walter runs toward the building.

"I'LL get it," Lawrence yells, running after Walter who makes it to the door first and opens it.

Fay struggles to get down. Norah assists her, allowing her feet to touch the pavement.

"I'll get it!" Fay repeats, wobbling and running toward Walter and Lawrence.

Norah looks around. "Thank you, Lord," she says.

"Come on, Mama!" Walter says, holding the door. Lawrence and Fay stand in the hallway. Norah walks in. The door slowly closes behind them as they hold hands and walk down the hall together.

...they hold hands and walk down the hall together.

About the Author

Shelonda Montgomery holds a Bachelor of Arts degree in English with a Creative Writing Concentration from Roosevelt University and a Masters of Arts in English with a Creative Writing Concentration from Southern New Hampshire University. Her works are in the journals *Sinister Wisdom, Akikiro, Prevention at the Intersections, The African-American Review,* and the poetry anthology *Urban Voices*. She writes for MyUmbrella.co and resides in Chicago with her son James and Grandmother Emma.

Enjoyed this story? Read more from Frayed Edge Press...

Literature

In Madison's Cave: A Novel by Douglas Anderson
Ambushing the Void short stories by James McAdams
*¿Cómo Hacer Preguntas? or How To Make Questions: 69 Instructional
   Poems (in English)* by Daniel Hales
Bellapalma by Jens Bjørneboe; translated by Esther Greenleaf Mürer
Ere the Cock Crows by Jens Bjørneboe; translated and with a
   reconstruction of the play by Esther Greenleaf Mürer
Right Guy, Wrong Time by Louise MacGregor
Stealing: A Novel in Dreams by Shelly Brivic
The Splooge Factory poety by Christina Springer

History and Politics

*"Do Not Misunderstand Me": The Collected Radical Addresses to the
   Unity Congregation (1888-1891)* by Hugh Owen Pentecost
Jeremiah Hacker: Journalist, Anarchist, Abolitionist by Rebecca
   Pritchard
A Nurse's Story: Medical Missionary in Korea and Siberia, 1915-1920
   by Delia Battles Lewis

Street Smart Series -- Short Fiction for People on the Go

Full Fare by Jean-Bernard Pouy
Down and Out in Paris, with Cat by R.A. Bolo
The Accidental Anarchist by A.R. Melnik
Stealing MacGuffin by Matthew Kastel
Pele's Domain by Albert Tucher
"Make the Bear Be Nice" by Stephen St. Francis Decky
The Day is Gone by Shelonda Montgomery

Visit us at: https://www.frayededgepress.com/

9 781642 510393